W9-CPF-360

BATTLE
OF THE
BOOKS

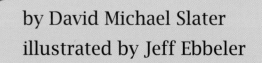

by David Michael Slater

illustrated by Jeff Ebbeler

magic wagon

visit us at www.abdopublishing.com

For Jace & Madelyn—DMS

Published by Magic Wagon, a division of the ABDO Group, 8000 West 78th Street, Edina, Minnesota 55439. Copyright © 2010 by Abdo Consulting Group, Inc. International copyrights reserved in all countries. All rights reserved. No part of this book may be reproduced in any form without written permission from the publisher.

Looking Glass Library™ is a trademark and logo of Magic Wagon.

Printed in the United States.

 Manufactured with paper containing at least 10% post-consumer waste

Text by David Michael Slater
Illustrations by Jeff Ebbeler
Edited by Stephanie Hedlund and Rochelle Baltzer
Interior layout and design by Becky Daum
Cover design by Becky Daum

Library of Congress Cataloging-in-Publication Data
Slater, David Michael.
  Battle of the books / by David Michael Slater ; illustrated by Jeff Ebbeler.
     p. cm.
  Summary: Two new books are dismayed when they are shelved at a library where the books judge each other only by their covers.
  ISBN 978-1-60270-655-2 (alk. paper)
  [1. Books and reading—Fiction. 2. Libraries—Fiction.] I. Ebbeler, Jeffrey, ill. II. Title.
  PZ7.S62898Bat 2009
  [E]—dc22

                                    2008055338

When the librarian fell asleep, a mystery novel approached Paige.
"Egads!" he said. "Wait till everyone checks you out!"

"Gosh, thanks!" Paige replied. She was new to the library and
thrilled to get such a warm welcome.

The mystery novel frowned at Mark, the other new arrival. "I'm afraid this library is all booked up," he said.

Paige was confused, but she always found mysteries a little hard to follow. She wanted to say something to Mark, but she'd only just met him.

Suddenly, the librarian woke up and set the books on a cart. Then she just as quickly fell asleep again.

"Is the librarian always so tired?" Paige asked.

"Always and all the time," said a thesaurus. "Every morning she has to re-shelve every book in the library."

"Why every book, every morning?" Mark asked, but no one would answer him.

The librarian woke up again and started pushing the cart. Paige and Mark forgot all about the strange behavior of the other books. They were in a real library! Tingles ran up and down their spines.

Paige was overjoyed by the friendly greetings she received. But across the aisle, no one was paying any attention to Mark. Paige considered calling to him, but there were just too many books to meet.

As soon as the library doors were locked that night, books began climbing down from their shelves. Confused, Mark and Paige followed and met on the floor.

"Where is everybody going?" asked Mark.

"Looky here, Dog-ear," sniffed a fashion guide. "We don't rub covers with just any books the librarian puts us next to. We re-sort ourselves the minute she leaves! Get it? Are we on the same page here?"

"So that's why she has to re-shelve all the books every morning!" Mark said. "Why doesn't everyone stay where they belong?"

"Do I have to spell it out for you?" cried the dictionary. "Look at yourself. Borrrrrring!"

"Now look at Paige," sneered the fashion guide. "She's the most gorgeous book I've ever seen!" And with that, the two books led Paige away.

"You get judged by your cover around here," a plain biography said to Mark. "But it's best that way. Just look at those fancy cover-lovers over there. Ha! Those kind aren't bound too tight, if you know what I mean."

"Not too much between the covers, if you know what *I* mean," a joke book added.

Mark was glad to be accepted at last, but something still seemed wrong. He wanted to get to know these new books, so he offered to summarize himself.

For a moment, no one replied. Finally, a book on manners said, "Um, I don't mean to be rude, but we don't do that."

"Then, how do you read each other?" Mark asked.

No one answered. They all looked away.

Meanwhile, Paige was being treated like a special edition. She knew it wasn't right, but she didn't know what to do about it. She decided to change the subject and offered to read her introduction.

Everyone looked horrified. For a moment, no one spoke. Finally, a rule book said, "Um, we don't do that."

"But . . . how do you read each other?" Paige asked.

No one answered.

Mark and Paige looked at each other. They were books and they wanted to open up, but could they risk it? They both looked at their groups again. Then, slowly, they walked toward each other.

Paige's group rushed out and tried to drag her away from Mark. Mark's group tried to drag him away from Paige.

The books kept pulling and pulling until Mark and Paige were about to be torn apart!

That's when Mark and Paige got the same idea at the same time. Together, they slipped out of their covers. At once, all the books in the library went crashing to the floor.

That's when the battle of the books began. It was all-out war.

The books charged each other. There were whoops and wails and then the terrible sound of tearing. Books were ripping each other's jackets off! In no time at all, not a book in the library had a cover.

Something amazing happened then. The books couldn't tell whom to talk to or whom to avoid. Then everyone noticed Mark and Paige. All this time, they'd been quietly reading each other, cover to cover.

It took awhile, but the dictionary started reading the thesaurus. Then the fashion guide began reading a poetry book. Soon, all the books were sharing their stories.

The books opened up to one another all night long. Before they knew it, they heard the doors being unlocked.

As quickly as they could, all the books hurried back up to their shelves—the shelves where they belonged.

The librarian came in and was shocked. For the very first time, all the books were right where she'd left them. She never felt so relieved—

Until she saw the floor that is! The books couldn't help but snicker.

IDIOMS IN BATTLE OF THE BOOKS

An idiom is an expression that means something different than the words would by themselves. Here are the meanings for some of the idioms in this book:

All booked up—full, with no more room

Checks you out—takes a look at you

Not too much between the covers—lacking substance

On the same page—understand one another

Recipe for disaster—a plan sure to fail

Spell it out for you—explain something entirely

ABOUT THE AUTHOR

David Michael Slater lives and teaches seventh grade Language Arts in Portland, Oregon. He uses his talents to educate and entertain with his humorous books and informative presentations. David writes for children, young adults, and adults. Some of his other titles include *Cheese Louise*, *The Ring Bear* (an SSLI-Honor Book), and *Jacques & Spock* (a Children's Book-of-the-Month Alternate Selection). More information about David and his books can be found at **www.abdopublishing.com**.